Twinkle

Twinkle

Akire Lynn Williamson

Copyright

Twinkle is a work of fiction. The names, characters, businesses, places, events, incidents and dialogue are drawn from the author's imagination and are not to be construed as real. Any resemblance to actual events or persons, living or dead, is entirely coincidental.

Copyright © 2017 by Akire Lynn Williamson. All rights reserved. This book or any portion thereof may not be reproduced or used in any manner whatsoever without the express written permission of Butterfly Typeface Publishing except for the use of brief quotations in a book review.
Printed in the United States of America.

First Printing, 2017

ISBN-13: 978-1-942022-95-4
ISBN10: 1942022956

Illustrated by JCBlue
Edited by JEM
Author Photo Courtesy of Maurice Gardner Photography
Interior Design/Layout by Iris M. Williams

The Butterfly Typeface Publishing
PO BOX 56193
Little Rock Arkansas 72215
(501) 823-0574

info@butterflytypeface.com

Be A Star!

for my family

Table of Contents

A Girl Named Aliya 14
Twinkle 16
Training Twinkle 18
Twinkle Goes To School 20
Star Class 24
Talking to the Stars and the Moon 26
The Makeover..28
Shape Shifting 30
The Battle of Naraby 34
The Shrinker..36
The Fairy 38
About the Author

Lesson 1:

Speak up!

A Girl Named Aliya

Once there was a girl named Aliya. She loved the moon and the stars so much that when she grew up, she wanted to go to outer space.
Aliya lived in a big beautiful house with her mom who was an actor and her dad who worked for NASA.
Aliya had many friends (Kiylaya, Naomi, Kira, and Kaya) and they all loved Math, Science, P.E, and Art.

Twinkle

One day, Aliya was looking at stars through her telescope and she saw the weirdest thing; there was something falling from the sky! It looked like a star!

Aliya went outside to see and sure enough, it was a falling star!

Aliya caught the star and took her inside to her bedroom.

To her surprise, the star could talk!

"My name is Twinkle," the star said. "I ran away from home because I was being teased for being the smallest star."

"It's ok to be small," Aliya said. "Be yourself and you will make friends."

"Ok," Twinkle said. "You have inspired me to not care about what others think. But, I don't know how to stand up for myself."

"Don't worry," Aliya said. "I will teach you how to speak up for yourself. I will train you."

Training Twinkle

Twinkle smiled and was very happy she met Aliya. The two began training right away in Aliya's room.

The first lesson they did was all about speaking up for yourself.

"You have to learn to talk back to the bullies. But never talk back to teachers or you will get into trouble!" Aliya told her new friend.

"OK," Twinkle said. "I get it. I must speak up and tell others how I feel!"

"That's good," Aliya said. "I know you are tired now. I can give you another lesson after school tomorrow."

"Ok," Twinkle said.

Twinkle Goes To School

The next morning, Aliya was up getting dressed for school.

"You stay here in my room Twinkle," Aliya said.

Twinkle did not want to stay there alone so she secretly climbed into Aliya's backpack. Twinkle was excited about going to school with Aliya.

At school, Aliya hung her backpack on her chair. In class, she learns all about English, Geography, and Equivalent Fractions.

Of course, it is Science that Twinkle enjoys hearing about the most!

Lesson 2:

Don't Become A Bully!

Star Class

After school, Aliya invites her friends over to play.

Twinkle decides she wants to meet Aliya's friends, so she suddenly jumps out of Aliya's backpack!

Aliya's friends are all SHOCKED to see Twinkle!

They had so many questions.

Twinkle told them about how the sun and the moon were married and that Earth was their third kid! Aliya's friends all agreed they had not learned that in Star Class!

Then Aliya told her friends how Twinkle left her home because she was being teased for being so small.

Talking to the Stars and the Moon

"Then you should say something bad about them!" One of Aliya's friends suggested.

"No," Aliya said. "You do not have to talk bad about others just because they talk bad about you."

Aliya's friends all agreed that talking bad about others was not a good idea.

Twinkle was happy Aliya was teaching her something so she decided to teach Aliya and her friends something too.

Twinkle told the girls that stars had their own way of talking to each other and they could also shape shift and become anything they wanted!

Twinkle taught Aliya and her friends how to talk to the stars and the moon!

The Makeover

The next morning, Aliya was getting dressed for school.

"Are you going with me today Twinkle," Aliya asked.

"No," Twinkled smiled. "I have something to do. It will be a surprise!"

While Aliya was at school, Twinkle shape shifted into a human and called herself Twinkle Washington. She practiced using her arms and legs. She even learned to write.

When Aliya got home, she was shocked to see the new Twinkle. "What did you do," Aliya asked Twinkle.

"I shape shifted," Twinkle said proudly. "Now I am like you and your friends."

Aliya and her friends gave Twinkle a makeover.

Shape Shifting

The next day, Twinkle went to school with Aliya.

During Star Class, the teacher taught them about shape shifting.

Twinkle had an idea!

"I will shape shift into a human and stay this way for the rest of my life," Twinkle said. "That way I never have to be bullied again by the big and evil Naraby."

Twinkle told Aliya that Naraby was very powerful and that no one could stand up to him!

Aliya was not afraid of Naraby. She also knew that what Twinkle was planning to do would never work. Aliya knew that Twinkle could not stop being who she really was.

"We must fight back and defeat Naraby," Aliya said. "I have a plan, but we must hurry to get to NASA. Naraby is a big bully and a jerk. But when we defeat him, he will cry like a baby and we will be heroes!"

Lesson 3:

Be Yourself!

The Battle of Naraby

Aliya, Twinkle and her friends arrived at NASA. There was the greatest weapon on Earth, the laser cannon. The girls had stickers and paint dots too.

"We don't want to look like savages in outer space," Aliya said. "Now it's time to make a spaceship so we can defeat Naraby and make history!"

The girls finished the spaceship and climbed inside. They made it to outer space just in time to spot Naraby and his henchmen.

"The laser cannons are very bright," Aliya said. "Grab a pair of goggles so you will not be blind."

The girls and Twinkle put on their gear and prepared for battle with Naraby!

The Shrinker

"Hello Naraby," Twinkle said loudly. "How are you doing?"

"I'm fine," Naraby replied. "Why do you ask?"

"Because there is a beam of light right behind you!" Twinkle said.

"There is," Naraby said and turned around to see.

"Launch!" Twinkle yelled.

Naraby stepped backwards right into the trap the girls had set for him. He fell into the shrinker and turned back into a normal sized star!

The Fairy

Suddenly a fairy in the shape of a star appeared.

"You did a great job," she said to Twinkle. "Now, I will make you as tall as Naraby was because you have saved all of the planets!"

Twinkle and the girls smiled because they were so happy.

"In your honor," the fairy said. "I will also grant you as the ruler of space and you will rule beside your dad the Sun! You deserve it!"

She waved her wand and POOF, Twinkle was now a big and tall star.

The fairy waved her wand again and made Aliya and her friends into honorary stars for the day.

That day they were all known as heroes!

"Don't Be A Bully. Be A Star!"

The End

About the Author

Akire Lynn Williamson was born July 3, 2008 in North Little Rock, Arkansas to Erika Ousley and Arthur Williamson. As a baby, Akire displayed gifted capabilities other babies didn't show. She developed a love for hearing stories, learning her ABCs, and watching television. As she grew, she became a wonderful big sister, nurturing her little sister and brother.

Once in Kindergarten, she learned to read and that love has continued to grow throughout her years at Tolleson Elementary school. There she excelled and blossomed into an honor student and an awesome friend.

As big sister, Akire started reading to her siblings every night. Then when she entered the 1st and 2nd grades, she began writing stories. From her love of writing stories, her desire to author books grew tremendously. She carries her journal with her at all times.

Now as a third grader at Murrell Taylor Elementary School, Akire's extraordinary talent will now be on display for the world to see with her debut book, "Twinkle."

Akire's family is very proud and supportive of the young author and know that this is only the first of many more publications.

Learn more about Akire by visiting her Fanpage on Facebook @AuthorAkireWilliamson

Tops of The Trees Books

An imprint of Butterfly Typeface Publishing

WWW.BUTTERFLYTYPEFACE.COM

Made in the USA
San Bernardino, CA
14 September 2017